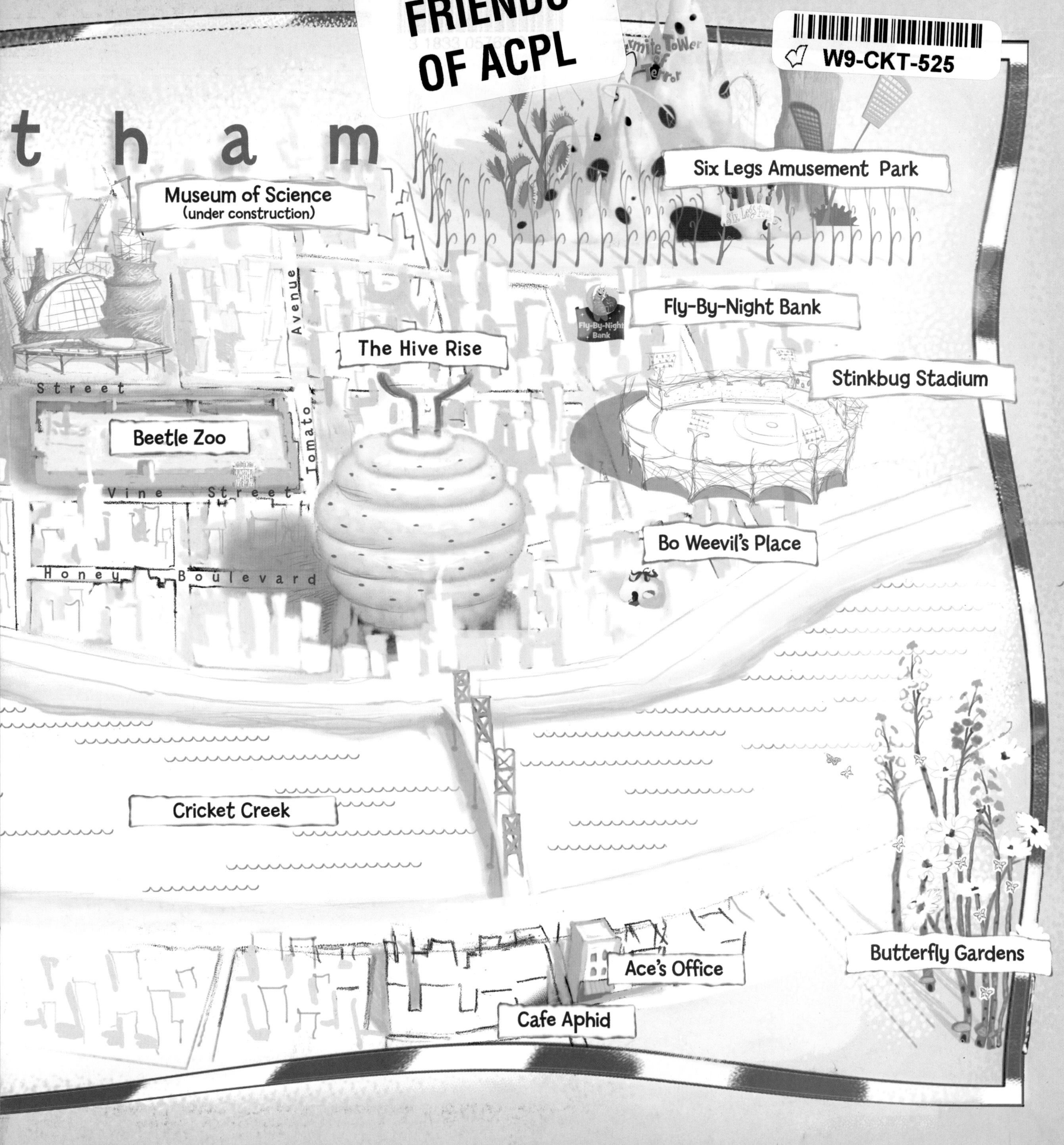
t h a m
Six Legs Amusement Park
Museum of Science
(under construction)
Fly-By-Night Bank
Fly-By-Night Bank
Avenue
The Hive Rise
Stinkbug Stadium
Street
Beetle Zoo
Tomato
Vine Street
Bo Weevil's Place
Honey Boulevard
Cricket Creek
Butterfly Gardens
Ace's Office
Cafe Aphid

Termite Tower of Terror

GRAND OPENING

Six Legs Park

Termite Tower of Terror Tickets

Front Entrance

The Rotten Apple

Please pardon our appearance. The park is still under construction

Keep Motham Clean. Don't Be a Litterbug

Some cases start small.

Some cases start big. This one started with a small flea with a big lump on his head.

The flea's name was Murphy—Scratch Murphy, the owner of Six Legs Park. He was itching to tell me something.

"I have a big problem, detective. I'm missing a lot of money I owe to a bank," said Scratch.

"How much money?" I asked.

"Enough money to build half of Six Legs Park," Scratch sniffed.

"That's a lot of dough you owe," I said. My gal Xerces and I listened to his story.

Scratch said that Six Legs Park was supposed
to open months ago, but some greedy carpenter
ants decided to quit before the place was
finished. They wanted better pay.

The flea had no choice but to borrow money.

The park finally
opened, and the flea
was hopping in cash.

This morning he stuffed his flea bag full of money and headed to the bank to pay the loan back. BAM! He got hit on the head with a carpenter ant toolbox. He woke up and the money was gone.

"Who knew you were going to the bank this morning?" I buzzed.

"Just the roach who gave me the loan, and my brother," he answered.

We took his flea-bitten case and headed to the bank.

The roach hissed hello.

I pretended I needed a loan.

"Are you from Madagascar?" Xerces asked.

"Yessss," hissed the roach, "and I'm going back tomorrow.
Too many bad bugs in Motham City for me."

"That's not a cheap trip!" I said.

"I came into some money by accident. A business deal," said the roach.

"What kind of business deal?" I asked.

"None of your beeswax," said the roach. "You still want a loan?"

"Nah," I said.

The roach wasn't talking, so we headed out the door. Was the roach the thief? Maybe the carpenter ant toolbox held some answers.

"It could be anyone's toolbox," the head ant said. "You know how many carpenter ants there are in Motham City? If you see one, there's a thousand more where he came from."

I asked the ants if they knew who might be out to exterminate Scratch Murphy.

CARPENTER ANTS
UNION
MOTHAM CITY LOCAL
No. 604

Termite Tower of Terror

Bo Weevil's COTTON CANDY

Hive Rise Honey

CAUTION HARD HAT AREA

"Well," said one ant, "it's tough getting rid of fleas, but a lot of ants around here would love to scratch Scratch out. And not just the ants. Why, Bo Weevil and Scratch argue all the time."

I know Scratch didn't want to get the police involved, but we needed to talk to Bo Weevil. Police Sergeant Zito "The Mosquito" knew Bo's neighborhood like the back of his wings. He also knew how to keep a secret.

Bo Weevil took his time coming to the door.

"Could you make it quick, detective? My larvae are in the middle of lunch."

We told Bo about the missing flea bag and asked him about his beef with Scratch.

"Sure, I'm mad," said Bo. "Scratch put my cotton candy stand right next to Queenie's Hive Rise Honey Stand. She makes the best honey in town. I can't sell any cotton candy when she's around. But Scratch won't give me another spot."

"I'm a family man, detective. Raising hungry little boll weevils isn't cheap. I'm closing my cotton candy stand and taking my business elsewhere. But if I were you, I'd ask Scratch's girlfriend a few questions. Maybe she took the money."

"Why's that?" asked Zito.

"Lady DeBug is a real beauty. But from what I heard, Scratch doesn't treat her like a lady . . . bug."

I looked at Bo's family. I couldn't recall seeing a cuter bunch of little boll weevils.

We took the Caterpillar to Six Legs Park. The place was swarming.

There was so much to do. We felt like little larvae again and almost forgot we were on a case.

We were on our way to the park office when I spotted a long-legged ladybug floating ahead of us.

"Ms. Lady DeBug?" I called out.

"What's this all about?" she said.

"Seems like someone was trying to play flatten-the-flea with your boyfriend," I said.

"Oh, my. Is he OK?" She looked worried.

"He looked OK to me, but I'm no doctor," I said. "He has a pretty big lump on his head and an even bigger lump of cash missing."

"Cash? Missing?" Lady's eyes narrowed.

"Did you know Scratch was going to the bank this morning?" asked Zito.

"No, he never tells me anything." She pouted. "But I did see him leave his office."

"Did you know about his bank loan?" asked Xerces.

"Scratch doesn't like to talk about money, and I don't like to bug him. He might be small, but he has a big temper. Now if you'll excuse me, I'm meeting someone, and I'm late."

Park Rules

1. Parents, keep your larvae with you at all times.
2. Please keep your antennae inside all rides.
3. Do not fly out of ride until it has come to a complete stop.
4. Don't be a litterbug. Keep the park clean.
5. Any unclaimed exoskeletons will be

We followed Lady DeBug around the corner and over to the Termite Tower of Terror. She stopped and waited. Then she waved hello to someone. That someone was Scratch. He gave her a package, and she put it into her empty suitcase. Then they walked away. Why didn't she say she was meeting him? And hey—what happened to the lump on his head? Where were they going, and what the—

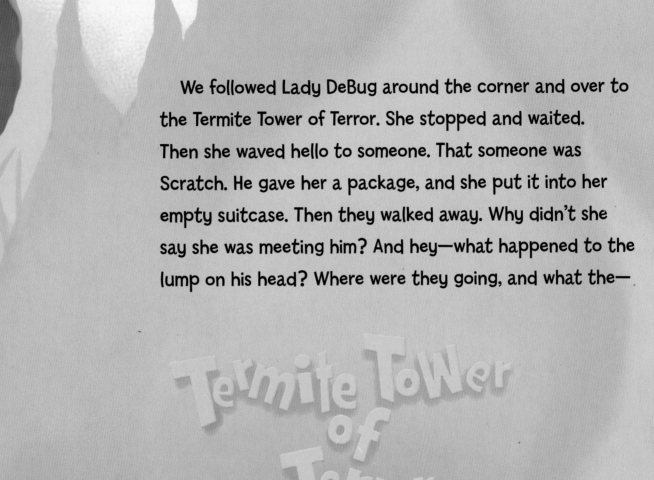

Termite Tower of Terror

Hive Rise Honey

Motion Sickness?
Try Queenie's New
Hive Rise Honey and Ginger
Termite Tower Tamer

We Accept
BEESA

Exit
Only

"Hey, detective, I've been lookin' all over for you." It was Scratch. "I've been thinkin', and maybe my—"

"Wait a minute," I interrupted. "Wasn't that you I just saw walking with Lady DeBug?"

"Wha—?" said Scratch.

"And you have a lump now—but you didn't just . . ." I stuttered.

"You saw someone who looked liked me," said Scratch.

"Someone who looked exactly like you," said Xerces as she touched his head. "Without a lump."

"My brother Scritch," said Scratch. "We're twins."

Six Legs Park Office

Authorized Bugs Only

We ran to catch up to Lady and Scritch. At the park office, Bo Weevil was coming out the door. He had closed up his stand for good and had just dropped off his keys. Scritch and Lady said good-bye to him and went inside.

"What do you think they're up to?" asked Xerces.

"No good!" yelled Scratch, his temper rising. He ran over and flung open the office door.

"What's going on here?" yelled Scratch as he burst through the door.

"We . . . um . . . ah . . . we . . . ah . . . " sputtered Lady.

"A woolly bear caterpillar coat! Who's this for?" demanded Scratch. "And isn't that my flea bag over there?"

Scratch picked it up. Only a couple of bills fluttered out.

"OK, where's the rest of the money?" asked Scratch as he looked at the fur coat. "Is this what you spent it on?" he asked Lady. "As if I wouldn't have bought you whatever you wanted. I can't believe my own brother and girlfriend robbed me!"

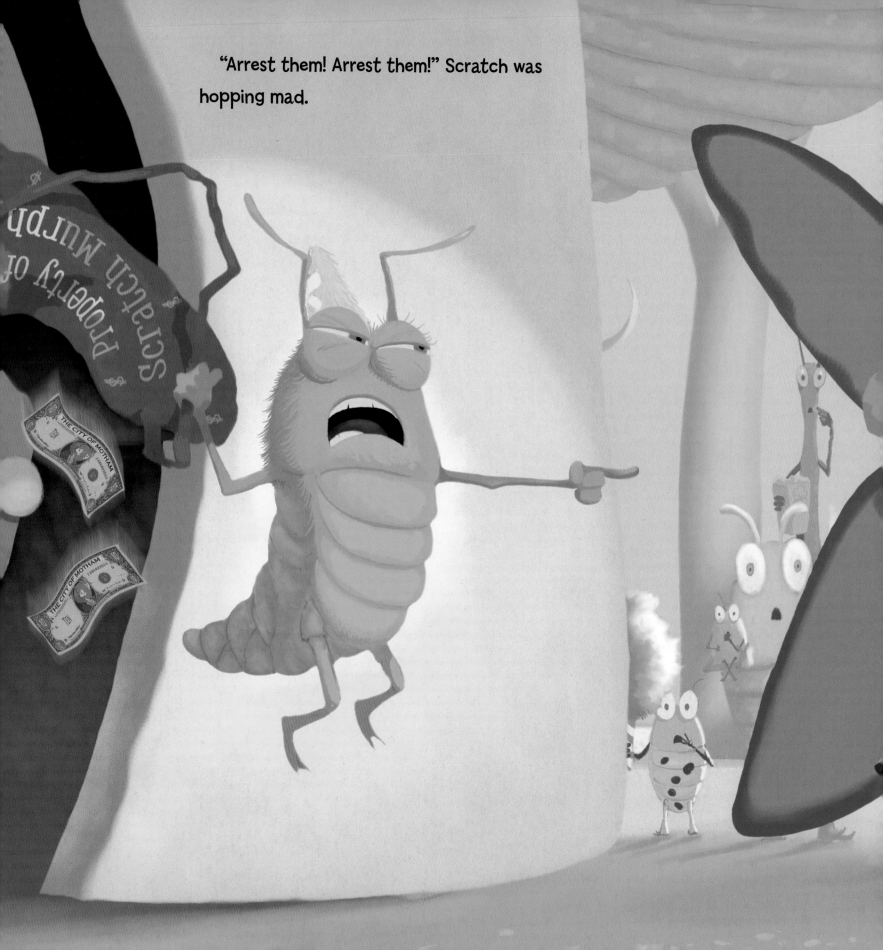

"Arrest them! Arrest them!" Scratch was hopping mad.

"No, you got it all wrong," pleaded Scritch.
"I don't know how your flea bag got in the office.
I didn't steal it! And the coat, it was a—"
"Don't say another word!" screamed Scratch.
The park police came and took the pair away.

"I've worked so hard to build this park.
I know a lot of bugs are jealous of my success.
But my own brother—my own family—and my
precious ladybug stole my money! I thought I
could trust them. DOESN'T ANYBODY LOVE ME?"
Scratch sobbed.

"It's all about family," said a voice behind us. It was Bo Weevil. "You don't have family, you don't have nothin'. Everything I need is right here," he said, pointing to his little family in their buggy. "Looks like you got your bad bugs, detective," he continued. "As for me, I'm taking the young ones out to a nice cotton field in the country. Gonna kick back and watch the little pupae molt and grow up."

He turned and walked away, shaking his head.

"What a family man that Bo is," said Zito. "You *never* see weevils taking care of their young like that."

My antennae twitched. Then it hit me . . . like a flyswatter.

"Family, schmamily," I said. "You never see weevils caring for their young because their babies grow up inside the cotton bolls and don't come out until they are adults! Those little weevils Bo's been carrying around—there's something not right with them. Bo's our bug, Zito!"

We ran after Bo, and he took off. A baby weevil fell out
of the carriage. It split open, and Bo's secret flew out.

Bo gave us a run for the money.

We brought the money back to Scratch. The park police had discovered that the caterpillar coat was a present from Lady that Scritch had helped pick out. Lady and Scritch had just been set free. Scratch turned to us with a tear in his eye.

"I've learned a lot today, detective," he said. "My family does care about me, and I need to control my temper. I'm making some changes. Anyone who works for me will earn a fair wage, and I'll give free admission to their families, too. Six Legs will be all about family and doing what's right and . . ."

Scratch went on and on as he walked away with Lady and Scritch.

The case was solved. Scratch had his fortune back,
and Zito was off to have his fortune told. As for me,
my fortune was in my gal's blue eyes.

Bo Weevil was never heard from again. Maybe he made it to that big cotton field out in the country. Maybe he didn't. But if he ever comes back to Motham City, I'll be waiting for him. Bad bugs are my business.

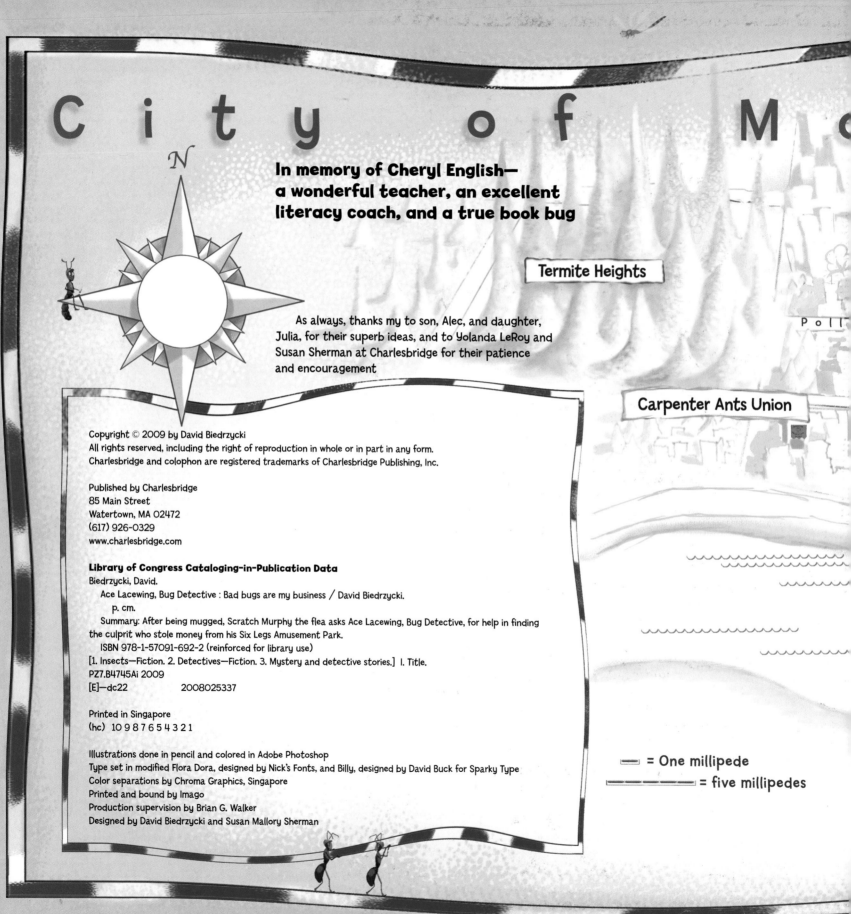

C i t y   o f   M

**In memory of Cheryl English—
a wonderful teacher, an excellent
literacy coach, and a true book bug**

Termite Heights

As always, thanks my to son, Alec, and daughter,
Julia, for their superb ideas, and to Yolanda LeRoy and
Susan Sherman at Charlesbridge for their patience
and encouragement

Carpenter Ants Union

Published by Charlesbridge
85 Main Street
Watertown, MA 02472
(617) 926-0329
www.charlesbridge.com

Library of Congress Cataloging-in-Publication Data
Biedrzycki, David.
   Ace Lacewing, Bug Detective : Bad bugs are my business / David Biedrzycki.
      p. cm.
   Summary: After being mugged, Scratch Murphy the flea asks Ace Lacewing, Bug Detective, for help in finding
the culprit who stole money from his Six Legs Amusement Park.
   ISBN 978-1-57091-692-2 (reinforced for library use)
[1. Insects—Fiction. 2. Detectives—Fiction. 3. Mystery and detective stories.] I. Title.
PZ7.B4745Ai 2009
[E]—dc22   2008025337

Printed in Singapore
(hc) 10 9 8 7 6 5 4 3 2 1

Illustrations done in pencil and colored in Adobe Photoshop
Type set in modified Flora Dora, designed by Nick's Fonts, and Billy, designed by David Buck for Sparky Type
Color separations by Chroma Graphics, Singapore
Printed and bound by Imago
Production supervision by Brian G. Walker
Designed by David Biedrzycki and Susan Mallory Sherman

P o l l

= One millipede

= five millipedes